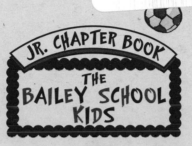

JR. CHAPTER BOOK

THE
BAILEY SCHOOL
KIDS

JR. CHAPTER BOOK
THE BAILEY SCHOOL KIDS

CAVEMEN DO DRIVE SCHOOL BUSES

by Marcia Thornton Jones and Debbie Dadey
Illustrated by Joëlle Dreidemy

SCHOLASTIC INC.
New York Toronto London Auckland Sydney
Mexico City New Delhi Hong Kong Buenos Aires

To Steve—we make a great team!
—M.T.J.

For Anna Singewald, Maryjo Faith Morgan,
and Fred J. Richart.
—D.D.

For Juju, my scary saber-toothed cat.
—J.D.

ISBN-13: 978-0-545-06989-2
ISBN-10: 0-545-06989-0

12 11 10 9 8 7 6 5 4 3 2   8 9 10 11 12 13/0

Printed in the U.S.A.
First printing, October 2008

CONTENTS

CHAPTER 1: AWAY GAME   7

CHAPTER 2: NED   12

CHAPTER 3: GAME ONE   17

CHAPTER 4: TIGERS   23

CHAPTER 5: CAVE ART   29

CHAPTER 6: LOSING STREAK   34

CHAPTER 7: FIRE   39

CHAPTER 8: MARSHMALLOW MADNESS   45

CHAPTER 9: BIG-TIME LOSERS   50

CHAPTER 10: CAT HUNT   55

CHAPTER 11: TEAMWORK   60

1

AWAY GAME

"Look at this," Liza
told her soccer team.

Melody, Liza, Howie,
Eddie, and the rest of the
second graders were on
the playground. They were
waiting for the bus to take
them to their first away
game. So far they had
played three home games.
And they had lost all of them!
Liza was the team manager.
She held up her clipboard to
show the team her notes.

Howie didn't look. He read a science book.

Eddie didn't look. He put a spider on Carey's head.

Carey didn't look. She screamed. And jumped. And screamed some more.

In fact, no one looked at Liza's ideas. Not even their coach. He was busy blowing his nose. He was too sick to care about soccer.

Melody was busy practicing her kicking. Melody loved to play soccer. More than watching TV. More than pizza. Even more than eating candy.

Melody kicked the ball. It flew across the playground and she ran after it.

Melody gave the ball another kick. It zoomed into the net.

Melody pumped her fists in the air.

She wiggled her hips.

She did a happy dance.

"That's good," Liza called to Melody. "Very good. But we need teamwork. Come look at this."

Just then Melody kicked the ball one more time.

WHOOSH!

It sailed through the air.

SMACK!

The ball hit Liza right on the back of the head.

2
NED

"I'm sorry," Melody said, running over to Liza. "Are you okay?"

"Yes," Liza said, as she rubbed the back of her head. Just then a bus rumbled around the corner. The brakes squealed like a wild animal. The bus jerked to a stop.

The door to the bus groaned open. "Hurry," Liza said. "We don't want to be late. But when Liza saw the driver she stopped.

The driver's head was hairy. His arms were hairy. Even his neck was hairy. Very hairy.

"Call me Ned," he grunted. "Ned Anderthal." He jerked his thumb toward the back of the bus. "On. Sit."

The team filed onto the bus and sat down. Howie opened his book as he walked down the aisle.

Liza looked at the bus driver. Even her Uncle Buck wasn't as hairy as the new driver.

Liza turned around and whispered to Melody, "Have you ever seen anyone with such a bushy beard?"

"It is pretty wild," Melody said. "Maybe he lost his razor."

"He looks like he's been lost in the woods for a thousand years," Eddie added.

Howie looked up from his book. "I hope he took a shower before he got on the bus."

Liza took a seat and looked at the back of Ned's head. It was hairy. Very hairy and very wild. Something about it seemed strange. Very strange.

3
GAME ONE

"No, no, no!" Liza yelled. "Stay in your spots."

But the team didn't listen to Liza. They all ran left. They all ran right. The whole team chased the ball in one big clump.

Melody got the ball. She raced toward the goal. But then Eddie ran into Melody. She fell into Howie. The three of them landed on Carey and Huey.

"Ow!" screamed Melody.

"Help!" yelled Howie.

"Get the ball!" called Eddie. But it was too late. The other team spread out. They passed the ball. They kicked the ball into the net. Goal!

That was their fourth goal.
Liza's team hadn't scored at all.

Liza shook her head. "I
wish they would listen to me,"
she said to herself. Liza's coach
just blew his nose.

Ned stood behind her and
grunted.

Liza turned around. "I didn't know you were there," she said.

Ned grunted again. "Soccer is wild."

Liza nodded. "Too wild. No one wants to stay where they're supposed to. Everyone wants to chase the ball."

"Just like tiger hunt," Ned grunted. "Must work together."

"Tiger hunt?" Liza said.

"Saber-toothed tiger," Ned said with another grunt.

"Oh," Liza said. She turned away from Ned just in time to see the other team kick the ball into the net. "Not again," she sighed.

4

TIGERS

"Nice try," Liza told her team as they got on the bus.

"It was the pits," Eddie said.

Melody nodded. "The other team killed us."

After everyone sat down, Ned started the bus. It moaned.

It shook.

It jerked to a start.

"Ned did say soccer was like a tiger hunt," Liza said.

"What does Ned know about tigers?" Eddie asked.

Liza nodded. "He hunted tigers – saber-toothed tigers."

"Cool," Eddie said. He used his fingers to make fangs. Eddie leaned over the seat and snarled at Liza.

Liza screamed.

AAAAH!

Ned jerked the bus to a
stop. He glared at Eddie in the
mirror.

"Oops, sorry," Eddie said.
"I got carried away."
Eddie sat down in his seat
and looked out the window.
Ned grunted, and the bus
started puttering down the road
again.
Howie patted Liza on the
back. "Don't worry. There are

no such things as saber-toothed
tigers."

"Yes, there are," Eddie
argued.

"Not anymore, there
aren't," Howie told his friends.
"They're extinct." Howie was the
smartest kid in second grade.
He knew all about animals that
weren't alive anymore.

"But Ned said he hunted
them," Liza insisted.

Howie shook his head. "There's no way. Ned would have to be a caveman to hunt saber-toothed tigers."

Liza didn't say anything. She looked at Ned's wild, crazy hair. It did kind of look like a caveman's hair.

5
CAVE ART

Liza shut her eyes to take a nap. She leaned her head back. Most of the other kids were busy talking to one another. Except Eddie. He sang a loud song.

99 bottles of pop on the wall... 99 bottles of pop...

Liza groaned. She knew she'd never sleep with Eddie singing. She opened her eyes. She couldn't believe what she saw on the ceiling.

Liza tugged on Melody's arm. "Look at those," she said.

Liza pointed to pictures on the ceiling. They looked like chalk cartoons.

One picture had people running all around. Next to that were pictures of people jumping. The last picture showed a pile of people on the ground.

Howie looked up at
the pictures. "They look like
hieroglyphics from ancient Egypt
or maybe cave paintings by
early cavemen."

Eddie stopped singing and
stared at Howie. "How do you
know about cave art?"

Howie held up his book. "I
read," he said.

Eddie grabbed for the book, but Howie knew his friend. He pulled it away just in time.

As the two boys wrestled with the book, Liza looked at the strange drawings. Then she looked at Ned.

"Cave drawings?" Liza said to herself. "Can it really be true?"

6

LOSING STREAK

"We're on a streak," Eddie said.

"A losing streak," Liza said. It was true. Their team still hadn't won a single game.

They were waiting for the bus to take them to their second away game.

Eddie grinned. "That means we're the number one losing team," he said.

Liza nodded sadly. Maybe if their coach wasn't still sick, they could win.

Eddie grinned. "We're number one! We're number one!" he chanted and started marching around the playground. Carey hopped in line behind him.

"We're number one!" they chanted.
Huey got behind Carey.

Soon, the entire team was marching behind Eddie, except for Liza, Melody, and Howie.

Liza sat on the ground and sighed. She didn't want to be number one at losing.

"Wait!" Liza said. "We need to talk about how we can win." But the team marched away.

"We'll never win if we don't work together," Liza said.

"At least they're marching together," Melody said.

"Here's the bus!" Liza called to the rest of the team. Eddie came to a sudden stop.

WHAM! Huey fell into Eddie.

BAM! Carey stumbled onto Huey.

SPLAT! Soon there was no line at all. Instead there was a big pile of kids on the ground.

BEEP BEEP

"Our team is just like those drawings in Ned's bus," Liza said with a sigh.

"What do you mean?" Howie asked.

Liza sat up straighter. "Don't you remember?" she said. "Nobody worked together in that drawing. They all ended up in a big pile. Just like our team."

Liza looked at her clipboard. She knew she could help the team if she could just get them to listen. But how?

7

FIRE

Nobody listened to Liza on the bus. Nobody listened as they got ready to play. Now the team was losing. Again. They ran after the ball like a bunch of bees.

"Stay in your position," Liza told her friends. But the team didn't listen.

Liza stomped her foot.
Liza jumped in the air.
Liza covered her eyes.

She couldn't stand watching her team lose. Again.

Ned wasn't happy about the game, either.

"Need pep," Ned told her after the game.

"Pep?" Liza asked.

"Bring team tonight," grunted Ned. "For pep rally." Eddie ran up beside them.

"Pep rally? Cool!" Eddie said. "Can we have a big fire?"

Ned grinned. "Like fire. Fire good."

That evening, the team sat around a big fire. Their parents huddled off to the side chatting. Ned stood by the fire, poking it with a huge stick. Sparks flew out of the flames.

"Teamwork! Teamwork!" Liza called out. Melody and Howie yelled along with her.

"We're the best!" Carey yelled. The whole team cheered along.

TEAMWORK!

Just then, Liza stopped cheering. She stared at Ned. He stopped poking the fire and swung the stick over his shoulder.

"Oh, my gosh," Liza called.

"What's wrong?" Melody asked. It was hard to hear above the cheering.

We're the BEST!

Liza pulled her friends away from the fire. It was chilly and she shivered. "Look at Ned."

As the other kids chanted, Ned danced around the fire. The clublike stick was still on his shoulder. His pants were ripped at the bottom, and he still wore a hairy vest with no shirt.

"He looks like something in a movie," Melody said.

Eddie laughed. "A caveman movie."

Liza looked at her three friends. "Only this is no movie. I think Ned IS a caveman!"

8

MARSHMALLOW MADNESS

Eddie laughed.
Eddie hit his chest.
Eddie yelled. "Me caveman, too!"

"Shhh!" Liza told him. "Ned will hear you."

Melody patted Liza's arm. "Ned is the bus driver. He can't be a caveman."

ME CAVEMAN TOO!

"Why not?" Liza asked.

Howie tapped his chin. "Maybe he's left over from the Ice Age."

"Don't be silly," Melody said. "Even if Ned was a caveman, what could we do about it? We can't even win a soccer game!"

Liza looked at the team. Three kids tugged on a bag of marshmallows. The bag tore.

Marshmallows flew through the air.

Huey had a spider in his  hand. He chased Carey and two of her friends. They raced across the playground screaming.

The coach just stood there, blowing his nose.

"We just need pep like Ned said," Liza said.

Liza raised her megaphone. "Who's the best?" she cheered. "We're the best! Go team!"

Liza waited for the team to join her cheer, but nobody heard. Eddie grabbed marshmallows off the ground. He started throwing them.

Plop.

One landed on Liza's head. "AAAAACK!" Liza screamed.

Plop.

Another marshmallow splatted on Howie's forehead. "HEY!" Howie yelled.

Plop.

A third marshmallow landed right in Ned's hairy beard.

"Oh, no," Liza gasped. "This is marshmallow madness! How are we going to play together if we can't even cheer together?"

9
BIG-TIME LOSERS

The team tried to play better. They tried on Monday. But Eddie kept tripping over Melody's feet. They tried on Wednesday. But Howie kicked the ball into the wrong goal.

MONDAY   WEDNESDAY

On the day of the next
away game, the bus rumbled to
a stop in front of the team.

The door groaned open.
Ned stood at the
top of the steps.
His arms were
on his hips. He
frowned. His eyes
were mad. He
pointed at Liza,
Melody, Eddie,
and Howie.
"You," he said.
"Get on. Sit down.
And no trouble!"

The four friends went to the very back. They slid down in their seats. That's when Liza saw the new drawings on the back of the seat in front of her.

"These look like us playing soccer," Liza whispered. "See how they're all bunched up like bees ready to sting?"

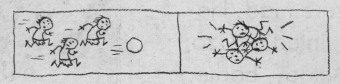

Melody shrugged. "You have to run after the ball to score," she said.

Liza didn't say anything else. She studied the pictures. Some of them did look like their team's worst plays. But other drawings looked very different.

At the game, Ned watched as the team played worse than ever.

Eddie kicked the ball away from Melody. Ned grunted. Huey tripped Eddie to get the ball. Ned stomped his foot. Ned looked madder and madder.

"Our team is losing big-time," Melody said during half time.

"Losing isn't the only thing we have to worry about," Howie said.

The four friends looked across the field at Ned. He frowned right back at them.

"Losing won't be as bad as riding home on a bus with an angry caveman," Howie said.

"I don't want to get back on the bus," Liza said.

"What if there's a new drawing and it shows Ned chasing a bunch of losing soccer players?" Eddie asked.

10

CAT HUNT

"Why DID cavemen draw on walls?" Liza asked.

Howie shrugged. "No one knows. Maybe to help teach kids. Or maybe to record things. Like how we write stories. But cavemen drew pictures instead."

"Like in comic books," Eddie said. "Only cavemen didn't wear tights. Or capes. Or fly after bad guys."

Melody laughed. "No, they grew their hair long and hunted cats with big teeth."

"I like that idea," Eddie said as he jumped in the air. "I'd be Eddie the Super Caveman."

Liza had her own idea. "Howie, give me your book."

"This is not a good time to do schoolwork," Melody said.

"There is never a good time for schoolwork," Eddie told her.

Liza looked at Howie's book. She pointed to a picture. "This is what we have to do," she said.

They looked at a picture of a cave drawing  in the book. Men with sharp sticks spread out around a large tiger.

"We have to catch a huge cat?" Melody asked.

"My grandmother won't let me have a spear," Eddie said. "I already asked."

Liza shook her head. "I'm not talking about that. I'm talking about winning."

Liza told them her plan. "If we spread out like these hunters did, we can block the other team."

Melody looked at the book. She looked at Liza. Then Melody patted Liza's back. "Liza, you're great!"

"No," Liza said. "Ned is." But her friends didn't hear her. They were too busy telling the rest of the team their plan.

11

TEAMWORK

"Hip-hip-hooray! Hip-hip-hooray! Hip-hip-hooray!" the team cheered.

"We won!" Eddie did a little dance.

"Thanks to Liza," Melody said as the team walked toward the bus.

"It's about teamwork."

HIP HIP HOORAY!!!

"You know a lot about soccer," Huey said.

"We should've been trying your ideas all along," Carey said.

"Liza was right," Melody said. "Soccer isn't about being the one who makes the goals."

"I didn't come up with the idea on my own," Liza told them as they lowered her to the ground.

"Who helped you?" Howie asked.

"Ned," she told them.

"NED?" Eddie blurted.

"Ned and his caveman drawings," Liza added.

Just then the door to the
bus creaked open. Ned walked
down the bus steps. His hands
were on his hips. His hairy face
frowned down at them.

Liza trembled.

Howie backed up.

Even Eddie looked scared.

But Liza didn't have to
worry. Ned smiled. He held
up a finger. "Number one!" he
said.

Howie pulled his friends off to the side. "If Ned really is a caveman, there will be more drawings showing what happened to us today."

The four friends walked to the back of the bus. They checked the walls and seats for new pictures.

Melody patted Liza's arm. "There it is," Melody said, pointing to a new one. It didn't have a big cat. It didn't have spears. It showed a team working together. Another one showed a very hairy bus driver dancing.

"That proves it," Howie said.

"Ned really is a caveman," Eddie said with a nod.

"What should we do?" Melody asked.

Liza smiled. "Nothing. Maybe cavemen DO drive school buses," she told her friends. "But in Bailey City, that's just fine!"